RECLAIMING SUNSHINE

THROUGH THE EYES OF A TYPICAL TEEN

KAVYA A

Made with ♥ on the Notion Press Platform
www.notionpress.com

The Kindness Foundation is a non-profit and kindness movement that is dedicated to promoting kindness, empathy, and compassion as the pillars of a better world. We run several programs, workshops and events year-round to not only inspire kindness in daily life but also create positive change.

The International Kindness Festival (IKF) is the first of its' kind global celebration of kindness. It is a platform where we share ideas, stories, and experiences that illuminate the path toward a world steeped in kindness.

We strongly believe that it is our youth who are poised to create positive change. The **Book Release event**, a part of the **International Kindness Festival 2023**, is a unique opportunity for our youth to share a piece of their soul through the written word and/or artistic expression, and get their work published. Recognising that being comfortable with your authenticity is a superpower and a form of kindness to self.

ACKNOWLEDGEMENTS

Maya Thiagarajan – Founder, TREE Learning
Diana Shathish – Art Educator & Entrepreneur
Notion Press Publishing

Contents

Prologue

Anticipating the future is a very tough job. Not even the most logical and shrewd brains can decipher this specific turn of events. Why? Doesn't science have answers for everything? Why? Aren't smart people the new brains of our society? No. The simple answer is no. The future is something that is unpredictable and somehow an unfortunate turn of events. We humans are free to live in the moment and just see how things turn out. But what if we have no choice but to grow up? What if the future is a place where we are not accepted? What will happen then?

Disclaimer

1

I ran to my room, crying. It had all come out now, and even though I was asked not to, I couldn't help it. I pierced down and tried to take deep breaths, though I couldn't find my phone. I searched my room for my phone, and there was the knife that might have started or ended it all. I walked towards it, and it just happened so quickly. My vision was blurred, my legs felt rough, and I couldn't breathe. I tried calling out for help, but my voice felt heavy and my hands were numb. It just happened in under a second. I just couldn't think. My voice sank, and I passed out.

I looked out the window, pondering the tiniest details of life. It was one of the most generic classes, and trust me, I wanted to pay attention. I did, but I just couldn't. My teacher was blabbering, and I didn't think she even cared if I was in the class or not. No one did. As I looked out, I thought about how the stillness of nature appealed to me. I could hear the wind and the way the trees swayed among the freeness of the gardens. I could see all the plants and shrubs at chest level with their fine, strong, resilient roots. The other plants and trees just merge with each other. It felt like nothing was out of place; everything belonged. Except for a beautiful, unbloomed flower. It was suppressed and turned away from the rest of nature. While the others had bloomed and had the most fascinating colours, this bud was rather different. All four corners of the bud were covered, and it was imprisoned and turned away almost as if it were ashamed of every single aspect of itself.

I could not stop staring at this flower. I wondered why this specific feature of nature appealed to me. Out of all the beguiling plants and flowers that had the most splendid colours, I related to this one. The suppressed, the most incompetent, and the most helpless one. That flower is me. I relate to that flower, as I know what it is. I can see why some people prefer the other plants over this. How it is ignored and not considered properly. My intrusive thoughts got ahead of me, and that was all I could think about. The class had ended, but my thoughts, emotions, and feelings from that specific period were still going on. The entire day, that day, I only kept saying to myself, "I know that flower. That flower is me." "I relate to that flower. That flower is me." because, at the end of the day, my imaginary and creative world is the only one where I'm allowed to be myself with no judgement whatsoever. I was flabbergasted at my own thoughts. My thoughts are like the wind. Sometimes too strong, sometimes too light. It comes and goes as it pleases, but it always has an impact on me. The day kept going on, and people kept talking about other things, but my mind was lost. I took a deep sigh and told myself to start focusing because I couldn't let anything distract me, especially before my studies.

I walked back to the classroom after a deep reflection on myself. I was feeling quite confident. I didn't understand why, but I was happy with it for the first time in forever. I decided to pay attention and listen to the teacher because we were discussing a topic I was quite familiar with. When we were having the question and answer round, the teacher asked us a simple question, which I knew the answer to. My heart raced, and my palms grew clammy as I raised my trembling hands, the universal signal that I wanted to speak. The room seemed to blur around me, and the noise of students' chatter transformed into a distant hum. She looked directly at me and asked me for the answer. Her tone made me wonder if she was surprised that I was finally contributing.

I desperately wanted to voice my thoughts and contribute to the discussion, but there was a knot in my throat, choking back the words. It was as if a part of me was suspended in mid-air, suspended between the fear of judgement and the burning desire to be heard. The seconds ticked by, and I could sense the expectation building in the room. Eyes turned towards me, waiting for me to break my silence.

I worked up the courage to share my perspective. Swallowing the lump in my throat, I mumbled the answer. As I sat there, having finally mustered the courage to answer the teacher's question, a mix of emotions flooded my mind. There was a sense of accomplishment for having spoken up, but it was overshadowed by the lingering discomfort I felt throughout the process. It was as if a weight had been lifted temporarily, but the fear of judgement still loomed in the background.

The teacher acknowledged my response with a nod and moved on to the next question. My classmates' attention shifted away from me, and the room returned to its usual state of bustling activity. However, my internal dialogue continued, dissecting every detail of the experience.

2

I was tired. I was tired of all the comments. Tired of school, tired of my family, tired of absolutely everything.

Today has been one of those days that feels like a never-ending battle against hurtful words and the overwhelming pressure to fit in. I wish I could say it was a rare occurrence, but it's not. The comments from my family and friends about my body size and my face acne have become a constant presence in my life.

The mornings are the hardest. As I stand in front of the bathroom mirror, I can't help but notice every blemish on my face. The spots that make me so insecure. The acne that seems to define me overshadows everything else. And it's not just my reflection that I see; it's the voices of those who have made me feel inadequate and insufficient. The images of people snickering right after they point at me. The ghastly comments are just replaying in my head. The world will move on, and time will continue, but these images will never go away. I wonder why my head is filled with daily comparisons and why they snicker and make jokes about my appearance. They never seem to stop, and it hurts me to bits.

But not only my classmates and those at school hurt me. My family, who are supposed to be my biggest supporters, don't understand how deeply their words cut. Their comments about my weight and appearance are like daggers to my self-esteem. It's as if they believe that by pointing out my flaws, they can motivate me to change. But all it does is reinforce the belief that I'm not good enough.

At school, the comparisons start. It's impossible not to notice the girls, who seem effortlessly beautiful and confident. They have flawless skin and bodies that fit society's narrow standards of beauty. I can't help but measure myself against them; every comparison feels like a reminder of my perceived shortcomings. They are built for the narrow mind of society, as they are perfect. Whether you are perfect or not, definitely entails multiple factors.

During lunch, I sit with a few people, but the fear of being judged keeps me from fully engaging in the conversation. I don't have friends; none of them are my friends. All of them would prefer one or the other over me. They don't understand the constant battle I'm fighting within myself. But I don't expect them to understand; after all, they're beyond perfect. They joke about their own imperfections, but it feels like they're in a different league altogether. I laugh along, but inside, I'm struggling to keep up.

After school, I go home, hoping for a respite from the criticism. But my family continues where they left off as if they've been keeping a running tally of my faults. It's disheartening to realise that the people who are supposed to love me unconditionally are the ones who make me feel the most judged.

Due to this never-ending situation, retreating to my room has become a routine. It's the one place where I can escape the relentless comments and comparisons. I lose myself in books, movies, and my devices—anything to drown out the noise of self-doubt that echoes in my mind.

But no matter how hard I try to avoid them, the parallels keep coming up. I'm overwhelmed with pictures of people who appear to have it all together when I scroll through social media. I keep comparing my behaviour to these crafted perceptions of reality, and

I always fall short.

I wish I could say that these comparisons have no effect on me, but I can't because they do; they impact me in even the smallest way possible. They undermine my sense of worth and make me wonder if I'll ever be adequate. It's challenging to escape this harmful thinking.

I've tried to build a facade of confidence, but it's fragile, and it shatters easily under the weight of others' expectations and judgments. It's a delicate balancing act between projecting an image of strength and crumbling under pressure. It feels like I am hanging on a thread. With each comparison, each target over my flaws, each snicker and laugh at my appearance, I slowly detach from this string, constantly struggling to hold on and move past it.

The weight of these constant comparisons and hurtful comments can feel suffocating at times, like an invisible burden I carry wherever I go. It's not just about dealing with occasional remarks; it's a relentless barrage that chips away at my self-esteem and leaves me feeling exhausted. It's a continuous pattern; neither does it stop nor does it get better.

As I lie in bed at night, I wonder if things will ever change. Will my family and friends ever realise the pain they're causing with their comments? Will I find the strength to confront them about how their words affect me? Will this ever happen, or am I getting ahead of myself?

I know that this battle against my self-doubt and the hurtful words of those around me is far from over. It's a journey filled with twists and turns, and there are days when it feels like I'm losing ground. Days were when my mind and my body just wanted to give up and go back to their normal state, where everything was once happy and everyone was once fine.

3

I was sitting on the bathroom floor. Right after an intense conversation with my sister. She made me realise that I can't just cry and whine over the imperfections of my body. It was a heated conversation, and voices were raised. But we didn't have a civil talk about these so-called imperfections and find solutions to resolve them. Instead, we fought. It was a huge fight. It all started when I decided to go into her room to talk because, years before she matured and became who she is right now, we used to be sisters. Getting-along-well-sisters.

I remember how we used to sleep together, and she told me stories about all the wonders of being a teenager.

My sister is 4 years older than me, so she always made me feel that becoming a teenager is one of the most joyful and elating experiences in the world. At least her teenage years are. She is the model daughter of my parents. According to them, I was supposed to look at her accomplishments and achievements and set myself up to live up to and pursue them. Firstly, because she is the oldest, all the expectations fall on her, but that doesn't matter to her because she is good at everything. And can keep up, unlike me.

Secondly, she always manages to bring me down. Sometimes immediately, although usually indirectly. I feel she wants to wave her achievements in my face to remind me that I am not capable of accomplishing anything. So, whenever we sit as a family when my parents ask us about our day, she never fails to mention that she got another perfect score on another one of her 'glorious tests'. Like always, my parents congratulate her and say things like "I've taught her so well" or "She is our daughter." It makes me imagine that if I got the same scores on that test, would they still say things like that? Or would they go ahead and make me feel as little and inferior as I already feel?

My sister is no better. She thinks the entire world revolves around her. If there is anyone who can make you feel like that, you are scanty and hopeless in almost everything. It's my sister. But there was a time when she was not like that.

There was a time when we didn't have to fight for our parents' attention, where having good marks was not a very big thing. Moreover, there was a time when she was considerate, made me feel so safe, and loved me to bits. If you take the previous picture of her and compare her with this version of her right now, you would think I am lying.

She doesn't care about me. At all. She doesn't even know that her actions and words make me feel so self-conscious. After all, I am like a nobody to her. Just a little dot in her distinguished life. Her good-for-nothing younger sister will bring about shame in her life and family. All these thoughts got the best of me as I was pondering about this when I was looking through all the old pictures saved on my laptop.

These pictures reminded me of all the best memories I had with my sister. How we used to laugh and smile together. How we were there for one another when the times were tough. I decided to speak with her. I knew it was a quick decision and required more thought, but at this point, I really didn't seem to care. Even though I did.

I slowly went to her room and knocked on the door. "Come in," she said. Steadily, with light footsteps, I opened the door and came inside. She was sitting on her bed, and like always, her head was buried in a very thick textbook. I could feel her eyes looking me up and down.

For the first few minutes, she asked me why I was there and what I wanted from her. I wanted to tell her everything—absolutely everything—but I could feel the lump in my throat forming again. It made me feel so uncomfortable that I wanted to remove myself from the situation as quickly as possible. "Why are you here?" she asked again. The weight shifted from my legs. I opened my mouth to speak, but no words could come out. "I wanted to tell you something," I said while stuttering.

"Tell me then." No matter how much I wanted to speak, words were not coming out. It felt almost identical to what I went through when I raised my hands in class. She then shouted at me, "CAN'T YOU SEE I'M DOING SOMETHING? I KNOW YOU WON'T UNDERSTAND CAUSE ALL YOU DO IS SIT IN YOUR ROOM, WHINING ABOUT HOW YOU ARE, AND HOW YOUR LIFE IS SO MISERBALE. BUT DO NOTHING AFTER THAT. BUT I'M DOING SOMETHING SO GET OUT."

My face turned red. I could feel my eyes watering. I looked at her with envious eyes, looking for even a hint of regret in what she had just said. I didn't find it. Her eyes were completely focused on the book, and I don't think she even realised how much of a big effect she had on me. I quickly turned around, slammed the door shut, and ran for my room. I knew it. I knew it was a bad idea. Why did I ever think she could change? Why am I always so naive? Things are nothing like they were before. I have given up hope. Her words kept ringing in my head. But I realised that if I couldn't talk to my sister, there was no one in the world that I could talk to.

I retreated to my room, tears streaming down my face and a

profound sense of isolation weighing on my chest. The photographs I had revisited earlier now felt like distant memories of a time when my sister and I shared laughter and friendship. Those moments seemed to belong to a different world, one that had slipped away quickly, out of my hands, leaving behind a void.

I permitted myself to grieve the past connection in the peaceful haven of my chamber. I questioned how we had come to this situation, where every interaction was tense and hostile. It was difficult to understand how someone who had once been my confidante and guardian had turned against me. How, with a period of time, and our own expectations and pressure, the distance between us had become too far, and neither of us was filling the gaps.

I yearned for my parents' assistance and not just my sister's but also their understanding. I wanted them to understand how damaging their words and deeds were to my sense of self-worth. I desired to be validated, to be appreciated for my own special traits rather than only as a reflection of those of my sister. But who would understand? Everyone was off in their own world, and I was just a tiny fraction of theirs. I wasn't someone you could be proud of or someone you could boast about to one of those Indian aunties during family functions. I was someone to whom everyone was ashamed and embarrassed to be related. I was a nobody. A huge burden.

It had been days, ever since the fight. My sister was not affected by anything like I had expected. For me, it was a wake-up call to reality. I know she is right. I am well aware that her comments are true. I do need to work on myself right now because, as I grow older, I will just start to lose more and more control over myself.

At school, I couldn't focus yet again on my studies. It was Friday. Friday is my favourite day of the week. Friday comes with a sign saying, 'It is the end of the week—one more week of putting up with torture; now take some rest.' Weekends are the best. No school, no putting up with the drawn-back insults and the snickers of those around in school. It was just two days of unwinding and relaxing. Usually, for me, it was like that. But ever since that conflict, I have been dreading getting home. In school, I never saw my sister, as we studied in different settings. But at home, I would have to put up with her and see her the entire time.

Even though we made no contact, my mind kept lingering over the fact that she had completely shut me out. All I could think about as I went along with the day in school was the fight that happened a few days ago.

My sister has always been blunt with her words. To her, there was no other way to say it. Her way of doing things is to be straightforward and truthful. I've had numerous conflicts with her before, but this time it was her saying something and me not raising my voice back.

Partly because I had lost my voice at that specific moment, and I didn't know how to get it back because of that disastrous and bothersome feeling and lump in my throat.

After school ended, I was experiencing conflicting feelings. I was dreading the time when I was required to see her at home for the next two days in a row.

Perhaps I could hide in my room like I usually do. Or just ignore her and let time heal the distance and big gap between us.

As I retreated to the sanctuary of my room, a familiar sense of solace enveloped me. The fading golden light of the setting sun streamed through the panelled windows, casting a warm and comforting glow upon the familiar surroundings. My room, once just a place to seek refuge from the world, suddenly appeared in a different light.

I began to notice the beauty in the simplicity of my space. The way my books lined the shelves stood as a testament to my curiosity and imagination. The soft hues of the artwork on the walls, each piece holding its *own story* and significance, The potted plants added a touch of greenery and life to the room, creating a serene ambiance.

Every corner of my room seemed to have a purpose, a place where I could retreat to be myself, away from the judgements and expectations of the outside world. It was a haven where I could reflect, gather my thoughts, and find a sense of peace.

Yet, despite the serene surroundings, my mind was still preoccupied with the echoes of our recent conflict. I couldn't help but replay the harsh words and tense moments that had fueled our argument. Though it was a small and quick dispute, those words left a big impact on me. The emotions that had surged between us lingered in my thoughts like ghosts refusing to fade away. I decided to take a rest because it was truly a tiring day and the circumstances could just get worse.

After a little break, I made the decision to turn to the calming warmth of my laptop to divert my attention from the chaotic state of my thoughts. I was determined to get away from the unfavourable thoughts and feelings that had taken over me.

As soon as I opened my laptop, I was immediately engrossed in a collection of adorable cat videos. Even on the gloomiest of days, they never failed to make me happy. As I watched their playful antics, I felt a gradual lightening of my mood. The laughter and innocence of these animals offered a temporary escape from the weight of my worries.

As I was feeling a little better, I stood up and made my way to the washroom, my reflection in the mirror beckoning me. As I looked at myself, I couldn't help but notice the acne marks that adorned my face. These blemishes, which I had often tried to dismiss as insignificant, now seemed to carry a heavier weight.

I kept hearing my sister say, "You don't do anything throughout the day," in my head. In a way, the acne scars represented both my perceived inadequacies as a person and the flaws in my skin. It looked like the world had stopped, and the ringing in my ears was just my sister replaying her words again and again. It appeared as though my fears and self-doubt were vividly displayed in the mirror's reflection.

As I focused on the marks more closely, I felt the tears welling up in my eyes again. It wasn't just about the physical imperfections; it was about the emotional scars that had been left behind by our argument. The tears flowed freely, a release of the pent-up emotions that had been building within me.

I immediately wiped away the tears coming from my cheek. With a newfound determination and confidence, I hastily walked back to my bed, closed all the videos, and decided to do research on my acne. I was sceptical of some of the ways to prevent acne, but trusting my gut, I went ahead with a few authorised ones. I was completely lost because I was so new to this. I also didn't have anyone to advise me about all the products I should and should not use.

I continued my research and decided to get a hold of myself. I would have probably spent a long time on the internet, just going through different articles and reports and looking for justifications to back up the content on specific websites. My head was bustling with facts, and I had finally come to a conclusion. I needed to take care of myself and remove all these imperfections and flaws that were holding me back in any way possible. All the information I collected was put in a notebook, and I made a routine. I wanted to imagine that everything was going to be alright and that I would finally love myself. I wanted to be one of those people who would accept themselves because they were happy with the way they were.

It felt like an impossible dream, and deep inside I knew it was. But I vowed that I would get rid of anything and everything holding me back. Even if it was in the harshest and most unreal way possible,

I made up my mind that these were the criteria that I needed to work on. The next morning, when I woke up, I decided to execute the first phase of my plan—to become productive and mindful of myself. I wouldn't say things were getting exactly better, but something changed in the way I thought. I was more positive. But like always, it was there for only a short period of time.

5

For the first time in forever, I woke up from my bed with a sense of purpose. I swung my legs and made my bed. I was happy and ecstatic, something I've felt after a long time.

It had been about a month since I embarked on my journey of self-improvement and self-acceptance. While the progress was gradual, it was undeniably there. The changes were small but significant, and I was happy with the fact that I was moving in the right direction. One of the most encouraging signs of progress was the slow disappearance of the acne marks that had long tormented me. The skincare routine I had adopted, along with a newfound commitment to a healthy lifestyle, was showing promising results.

I had read countless articles and numerous YouTube videos. With each piece of information I absorbed, my confidence grew, and I became increasingly convinced that my chosen methods were going to work. As I went about my day, a smile seemed to have permanently affixed itself to my face, and I even made the effort to talk to a few of my classmates.

Not the people who made me second-guess every step of my life or the people who constantly made remarks about my beauty and my body. The ones who never had anything against me and the ones who never made a remark or a comment on my appearance are the people I made an effort to converse with, even though I was scared at every interaction.

Even my communication was improving. I could interact with my classmates with only a few stuttered words. My attitude towards so many things was getting better, and I have to say, those were a few of the reasons my acne marks started to slowly fade.

Back at home, I had tried those remedies, and for a long time, I didn't hear any sort of comment from my family. Mainly, one of the reasons was that I didn't think to spend so much time with my family, as my key area of focus was myself.

Slowly but steadily, my pursuit of self-improvement had transformed into an addiction. I couldn't stop researching and purchasing products for my skin—supplements and other materials that might help me achieve my desired results. I pushed myself to the point of exhaustion, believing that if I just worked harder, I would see faster progress.

My primary focus was on self-improvement, and I was absorbed by it. What had initially started as a simple goal to take better care of myself and my skin had turned into an obsession.

I spent hours on different sites and on multiple compositions, all for one motive: self-care. I can no longer recognise myself. It's as if I've set out on a journey into the depths of my insecurities, and I'm lost, unable to return.

The more I fell into this obsession, the more I distanced myself from my family. While I had initially sought self-improvement as a way to boost my self-esteem and well-being, it had unwittingly taken me away from the people who cared about me. My singular focus on my skin and appearance had isolated me from the very support system that could have provided comfort and understanding.

I wanted it to be over—all the pain, suffering, and countless nights

I had spent on the internet. I had also become increasingly cautious about my weight, but I lacked an ideal or primary source to guide me. All of the sites and magazines I had read drew me back to one conclusion: I should eat less. It showed me people who ate and consumed less food were not gaining weight. As a result, I resorted to starving myself, believing it would help me fit the dimensions of a normal scale. Little did I know that I would lose myself in the process.

I can vividly recall how it all began. The various scenarios played out in my mind, causing me to question whether I should have even started this horrendous method of losing weight. I was constantly hungry, yearning for a moment of relaxation and acceptance of my own body. However, no matter how much I tried to convince myself that it was just for one more day, I knew deep down that I would keep repeating this destructive cycle.

The weight of societal expectations pushed me to embark on this plan, but it became increasingly difficult for me to keep up. Every step I took, every video I watched, every article I read—they all seemed to serve a greater purpose, one that I thought I understood. But clearly, I was mistaken.

My family was also slowly catching on and realising all the measures I was taking. They were concerned about my health and my attitude towards my body. My parents had asked me three to four times about what I was doing. They expressed sympathy, asked me to eat, and advised me to stop whatever new methods I was using to lose weight. But my quest for perfection made me blind. I was hurting myself physically and emotionally, but I was blind to it.

I spent hours in the bathroom, looking at the mirror, applying all the products that were now surrounding the bathroom floor harshly. It seemed that with every flaw I tried to hide, more of them were slowly uncovered. My mind felt suppressed, and I spent days on the internet as well as sleepless nights. My head was hurting, and my hunger was worsening. It was painful. I didn't know why I was doing this anymore. WHY? I asked myself. It is not making me happy. WHY don't I see a drastic change? WHY?

6

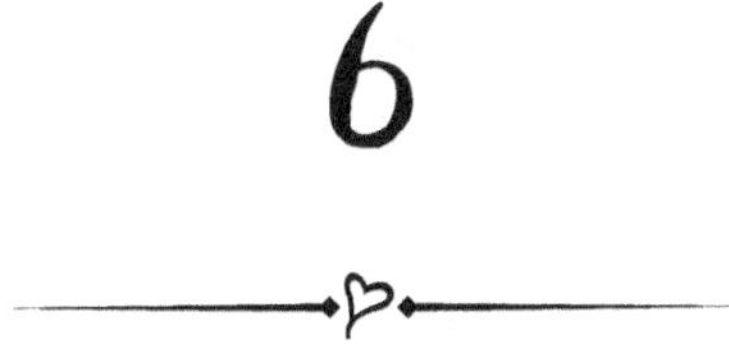

I was anxious. Though some of my methods worked, a few of them had failed, and a few of them had yielded ruthless outcomes. Today was the day when I had to meet the rest of my family, especially my grandmother. My household is no different than others—the same Indian aunts and uncles—a typical Indian family.

Whenever our family gathered, the conversation invariably revolved around each individual's well-being. It was during these gatherings that I endured countless rude comments, snickers, and muttered remarks. These hurtful words played a significant role in shaping the person I had become. My relentless obsession with achieving thinness and striving to eliminate every acne mark from my face was a direct result of the criticism, especially from my family and, to a lesser extent, my classmates.

I am supposed to meet my entire family today. I wanted to show them that I have become more productive and that I've finally started working on myself. So instead of sulking and whining about meeting my family, like I usually do, I wanted to be confident and have the power to show them that I too can change. Maybe if I showed them I had changed, they would consider my feelings and my concerns.

I heard the bell ring, and I hurried to the door and opened it. My grandparents, my aunt, my uncle, and my cousins were at the door. I welcomed them in, and while everyone settled, I helped my mom bring out the glasses of water. My entire family had made themselves comfortable and were laughing and talking amongst themselves. When I came out with the water, I slowly kept it down and touched the feet of my elders.

I sat down in the place left, and we all just continued talking. My grandmother then asked both me and my sister about how our school was going. I was about to open my mouth, but my sister decided to overstep and speak first. She started talking about how she got a special appreciation note from her teacher. Then she moved on to her studies and how she was on top of her class and got good marks in all subjects. All of the elders in my family, including my aunt, looked at her with approval, nodded their heads, and smiled at her.

I was already dreading my turn to speak. Nothing had even happened yet, but that familiar sense of dread had already enveloped me. After my sister had finished her round of indirect boasting, my grandmother turned her attention to me and inquired about how my school was going. My grandfather gave me a full, wholehearted smile, and my heart melted as my gaze became more confident. I lifted my body up and sat in an upright way.

Summoning my courage, I looked at my grandparents and the rest of my family. "My grades are satisfactory," I began. "I don't have the worst marks." My eyes kept shifting towards my aunt, who had a history of making comments about my insecurities.

As I spoke, I could feel the weight of their expectations and judgements bearing down on me. It was as though every word I uttered was being scrutinized, dissected, and evaluated by my family members, especially my aunt. Her presence alone was enough to make me self-conscious.

When I met her gaze, she gestured towards my legs and bluntly remarked, "You're still on the heavier side." Gathering my composure, I replied, "I've begun prioritising my health and well-being more." Curious, she probed further, asking, "How long have you been on this health journey?" With a hint of satisfaction, I responded, "It's been a month now, and I feel positive about my progress."

My aunt laughed.

My face flushed. My grandmother saw me turning red and immediately interrupted my aunt. She changed the topic and was slowly taking everyone's eyes away from me as I fled the room. My grandfather gave me a reassuring look and took part in the conversation, but it wasn't enough.

I quickly went up the stairs and into my room. I walked to the bathroom and stared at myself in the bathroom mirror. I ran my hands against my face; the acne marks and their uneven texture were a constant reminder of my insecurities as I pricked my nails against all of them.

JUST GO AWAY, I thought to myself. No matter how much I tried, someone or the other would keep reminding me about all my insecurities. I just never thought it would be my own family. I sat down and began crying. Covered by all the products, I realised that I had been too obsessed with my skin and even my body. I knew that if I wanted to be healthier, I shouldn't starve myself; instead, I should just reach out for help, distract myself, and be more mindful. I knew that despite all the circumstances I was going through, I still had my grandparents.

I went down again, tiptoeing, so nobody would notice that I was back. Not that anyone cared anyway. My family was sitting at the dining table now, except for my grandmother and grandfather, who were still sitting on the sofa. She gently called me to her side, and

I went, knowing that I would feel comfortable around her. They made me sit in between them and told me a story about a girl who had the same problems with her face and her weight as I did. She told me that the girl slowly flooded and distracted her mind with the things she loved to do most.

In addition, she only had a few steps for her skincare and tried old-school remedies that worked for her skin. Moreover, she exercised every day and didn't have to give up on her food. As my grandmother was continuing with her story, I couldn't help but wonder who this was about. My grandfather kept making signals to my grandmother upon seeing my curious face. I smiled. I was glad that she could relate and not make comments like other people usually do.

My grandma then smiled at me and said, "You should love yourself; however you are, Ruhi, you are beautiful." I hugged my grandma and smiled at her. My grandfather said, "You are still a child he fabricated. No need to take matters to your head. It's really important you stay calm and collected, okay? And your dadi and dadu will always be there for you!" I looked at him, and I felt so happy.

I could not thank them enough for always being there for me, right when I needed it. These were the moments that made me realise that my family was one I cherished and loved to bits. I would hold on to these intricate and special moments, without a sense of regret and disregard.

With the words of encouragement, I reflected and thought about what they had said. I decided to take it slowly, one day at a time. I didn't realise at that time how much this must have helped me.

I knew what I needed to do. While I felt some uncertainty, I understood the necessary steps I had to take to regain my well-being. I had come to realise that the extreme measures I had taken before were misguided. I had been so focused on the idea of "fitting in" and "taking care of my appearance" that I had lost sight of everything else—my studies, my time, and my overall well-being. It wasn't the path I had hoped for, but it was where I ended up.

After this abrupt awakening, I found solace in opening up to someone, in sharing a hug, and in listening to the comforting words of my loved ones. Opportunities like that seemed rare now, and I was determined to make the most of them. I wanted to carefully chart my course, aiming for a future that was healthier and more fulfilling.

The comfort I found in talking to my grandparents was incredibly appealing, and I yearned to find someone who would listen to all my concerns, share their experiences, and provide guidance, much like they did. I began piecing things together and realised that I needed to seek the help of a therapist. It was time for me to take this important step towards healing and self-improvement. I knew that it was a significant decision. It wasn't a sign of weakness but rather a courageous step towards taking control of my life. I had learned that seeking help was a sign of strength.

The terms "therapy" or "therapist" were uncommon in my cultural community. Not many people were aware that there were professionals out there who were willing to lend an empathetic ear, provide practical advice, and offer logical solutions to life's challenges. The issue at hand wasn't whether or not a therapist could be helpful, but rather gaining my family's approval for such an idea and addressing the financial aspect of it.

In my culture, seeking help for mental health concerns was often stigmatised or simply not discussed. It was important for me to bridge the gap between my family's traditional beliefs and the modern understanding of mental well-being. I knew that introducing the idea of therapy might be met with resistance or scepticism, but I also recognised that it was a crucial step towards my personal growth and healing. As I pondered how to approach this delicate conversation with my family, I reminded myself that taking care of my mental health was a valid and essential endeavour.

As I dove deeper into researching the benefits of therapy, I became increasingly convinced that it could work wonders for me. I was determined not to let the idea be dismissed, as it had been when my sister mentioned it. So, I devised a plan. My first step was to raise awareness and help my family understand the potential advantages of therapy. I knew that not everyone would immediately grasp the concept, so I wanted to present them with concrete, practical information.

I knew that in a few days, my family would come to my house. I wanted to execute my plan then. It would be very intriguing and helpful to talk to someone who had gone through similar experiences, but I just thought my family should know.

It was a very practical decision, but I clearly disregarded the amount of money and cost that was going to be put into this resolution. I thought I would leave that up to my family, most probably my parents. That was a field they could share their opinions in, and I would feel more comfortable if they did that.

I had carefully planned everything, and I really needed this. My past behaviour was a reflection and an example of how badly I needed to experience such a helpful and beneficial circumstance. I had a deliberate plan, and I was determined it was going to go well.

Days passed, and I had finally reached the point where I would be able to share my thoughts and voice my desire for help.

Once again, my grandmother, aunt, uncle, and cousins were sitting on the sofa, looking at me as I began to speak.

I wasn't nervous; I just had a sudden surge of confidence and determination because I knew this specific activity could do a lot of good for me. I had started out with a faint and rather soft voice, but I was reminded once again that the people that I loved were there and no one else. My grandparents were also really helping by not glaring like the others but instead smiling and helping me throughout this situation.

I was finally done talking, and everyone discussed. My parents were looking at each other, and my sister looked offended that my family was even considering therapy for me. My grandparents were looking at me, smiling, and I instantly felt better, moving away from the delicacy of the mindset that my family would want anything bad for me.

My mom began to say, "We never considered therapy for Esha, so why should we do it for you?" I told her that before, Esha didn't provide proper reasoning for her need for therapy; she just said she would love to talk to someone who could help her out. But I really need it, I continued to say, looking at my sister.

As I looked around the room, I could feel the tension building. I noticed a few eyes glancing at Esha and then back at me. I knew that I shouldn't have taken advantage of the moment there, but I couldn't help it. Esha hadn't really prepared for her case, whereas I had taken the time to gather information, research, and understand how therapy could truly benefit me. I was more determined than ever to start therapy and make a positive change in my life.

Anticipating all of their answers, I asked in an impatient tone if they were all okay with it. My parents looked like they were going to give me the signal to go ahead with my new ambition to take part in such a wondrous programme when my aunt unexpectedly stepped in. She laughed, not softly but really loudly. It was a laugh that seemed out of place in this serious discussion. I knew she was making sure that I and all the other members of our family would hear her and question her motive.

But this time, she didn't even give anyone a chance to speak. She simply got up and said, her voice dripping with disdain, "This girl is trying to take more money out of your hands. She has already spent a fortune on her face products. These useless therapy sessions also cost a fortune." Our ancestors never needed such luxuries, and they turned out just fine.

Sending her to school and giving her a proper education is all she needs. These so-called therapists are just in it for the money, preying on vulnerable people like her. She's just going through a phase, like we all did in our youth.

It's a part of growing up, nothing more." Her words hung in the air, casting doubt and uncertainty over the room as the family members pondered her argument.

I could feel the anger and frustration bubbling up inside me, a volcano of emotion threatening to erupt. I wanted to say so much to her—to defend myself and make them understand. But I held back, biting my lip so hard that it almost bled. Her words stung, and it seemed like she had already convinced my dad. It was true that I had invested quite a bit in my skincare products, but this time, I knew that therapy could impact my life for the better.

As the tension in the room grew thicker, the weight of their disapproval bore down on me like a heavy storm cloud. One by one, everyone at the table agreed with my aunt. Their disapproving glances and hushed murmurs crushed my hopes. They didn't seem to have any faith in me, and especially not in the power of therapy. I had hoped they would understand and support my decision. It was for my well-being, for my sake, and I didn't expect my own family to oppose what was best for me.

Frustration and disappointment welled up inside me, threatening to consume me entirely. I couldn't contain my emotions any longer. I slammed my laptop shut with a deafening crash and stormed off to my room, as the weight of my laptop was sinking in my hands. The sound reverberated through the house, a stark declaration of my anger and defiance.

At that moment, I felt a huge pang of anger towards my aunt. While I knew that respecting one's elders was important, at that time, I just couldn't think straight. It felt like she was determined to make my life miserable, and I was caught in the middle, suffering and desperately searching for a way out in the midst of this emotional storm.

It was one of those days at school where I couldn't pay attention. The classroom was buzzing with the usual energy of high school students, but I was somewhere else entirely. My mind had wandered off into a tragic yet bearable mindset, lost in thoughts that had nothing to do with the math lesson unfolding in front of me. The rhythmic drone of my teacher's voice seemed distant, like background noise in a world of my own making.

The sharp call of my name snapped me back to reality. My heart pounded as I realised that all eyes were on me, including those of Mrs. Anu, my stern-faced math teacher. The sudden silence in the room was deafening.

"Um, sorry?" I stammered, feeling the flush of embarrassment creep up my neck.

Mrs. Anu raised an eyebrow, her gaze unwavering. "Ruhi, could you please share with the class what you find so fascinating that it takes precedence over today's lesson?"

My cheeks turned pink as I fumbled for words. I hadn't been paying attention, and now I was being called out in front of everyone. It was a situation I had always dreaded, and it was happening right before my eyes.

"I was just thinking about something," I mumbled, my voice barely audible.

Mrs. Anu's lips curled into a tight, disapproving smile. "Thinking about something, Ruhi? In my class, we're supposed to be thinking about math. Would you care to enlighten us on the nature of your thoughts?" She said it in a slightly harsher tone.

I sank lower into my chair, desperately wishing for the moment to pass by or for the class to start talking again. The laughter and whispers of my classmates were like daggers, and it felt as though all the oxygen had been sucked out of the room. I had become the centre of attention, and it was a spotlight I never wanted to be under.

I yearned to leave the situation. I knew that if I denied the fact that I was paying attention, I would go deeper and deeper into the spotlight. I wanted to retreat, and the best way to do it was to apologize. "I'm sorry," I mumbled, unable to meet Mrs. Anu's gaze. "I wasn't paying attention."

Mrs. Anu sighed deeply, her patience wearing thin. "Ruhi, it's crucial that you pay attention in class. We are here to learn, and that requires your active participation. Please try to stay focused, and if you can't, remember there's always the option of staying at home." Her words carried a harsh reprimand.

Nods of understanding and a few stifled chuckles rippled through the classroom as Mrs. Anu resumed her lesson. I could feel the weight of my classmates' eyes on me, and the embarrassment burned hotly within me. I had always been a quiet student, preferring to blend into the background rather than draw attention to myself. Now, I was painfully noticeable.

As the lesson continued, my cheeks remained flushed, and my mind struggled to concentrate on the material. Every word from Mrs. Anu felt like a reproach, a reminder of my inattentiveness. I couldn't help but wonder if she had singled me out deliberately or if it was just an unfortunate coincidence. Either way, the damage was done.

The bell finally rang, signalling the end of the class, and I couldn't escape fast enough. I gathered my books and hurriedly made my way to the door, avoiding eye contact with my classmates. I could still hear snippets of their hushed conversations and their amusement at my moment of embarrassment.

Once outside the classroom, I leaned against the wall and took a deep breath, trying to steady my racing heart. I felt humiliated, like I had a giant spotlight shining on my shortcomings. The fear of being ridiculed and judged by my peers had always been a shadow lurking in the corners of my mind, and today, it has come true.

The rest of the day passed in a blur. I went through the motions of attending my other classes, but I couldn't shake the lingering embarrassment from that morning. I knew it was just a harmless interaction, but it was the first time the spotlight was on me and just me alone.

I was standing next to my bag, taking out my books, when my classmate joined me. She approached me and, in an annoyed tone, told me to go meet Mrs. Anu in her office because she had called for me. I tried asking her why, but she turned away hastily, impatiently reaching for the exit, clearly not making conversation with me any longer. I did not know why she had called me to her office; maybe it was because of the disheartening conversation we had.

My heart raced as I found myself walking through the corridors and right outside the teacher's lounge, which now seemed empty. I knocked and was summoned to Mrs. Anu's desk. The morning's embarrassment still hung heavy in my mind, and I couldn't shake the feeling that she was going to address that specific incident.

With a soft but anxious smile, I cautiously approached her desk. Mrs. Anu was leaned over, absorbed in the act of writing something on a piece of paper. She didn't take her eyes off the note, even when I came in, but acknowledged me with a slight nod. I drew closer to her desk, my footsteps seeming rather unnaturally loud in the hushed space near her desk.

I was standing right in front of her desk, waiting for her first sign of communication. Mrs. Anu finished her writing, carefully folding the paper and sealing it within an envelope. She looked up, her stern expression softening as she noticed my apprehension. Her eyes held a glimmer of kindness, contrasting with the earlier sternness that had sent me reeling in the morning. It was a surprising shift in demeanour that piqued my curiosity about the contents of the sealed envelope.

Mrs. Anu's gaze softened as she looked up at me. "Good afternoon, Ruhi. I know you might be wondering about my sudden request for you to come here, but rest assured, I just want to discuss your academic performance with you," she began, her voice gentle yet serious. I nodded, my heart still racing from the unexpected summons.

"So, Ruhi, as you know, you are usually an excellent and diligent student. I've never encountered any significant issues with your academic progress. However, lately, I've noticed that you've been falling behind," she continued, her words weighing heavily on my conscience.

My eyes grew wide open. I am genuinely shocked now. I didn't notice that I was falling behind. I just thought that my daily ponderings were just affecting my attention in class. Now, I realised I might have been taking it too lightly, and the implications were sinking in.

I took a deep breath, feeling my voice waver slightly. I stepped closer to her desk, my sincerity evident in my apology for my inattentiveness. She regarded me for a few moments, her expression thoughtful, as if she were deliberating something important. Finally, she whispered softly, "All is well. Could you please take this note to your parents for me? Make sure they read it before you do, and deliver it in the same manner I'm giving it to you."

"Yes, I will," I replied earnestly before she dismissed me. As I walked back to my classroom, a feeling of unease settled over me. There was something amiss, though I couldn't quite pinpoint what it was.

Later, when I returned home, I handed the sealed note to my parents, emphasising that it was intended specifically for them by Mrs. Anu. I wanted to disobey the very straight-forward orders she had given me and open the note to rid my thoughts of all the predictions pertaining to this certain note. But that was going against my morals and all the principles taught to me. I left it at that. I would find out anyway; I just didn't know how soon I was going to find out.

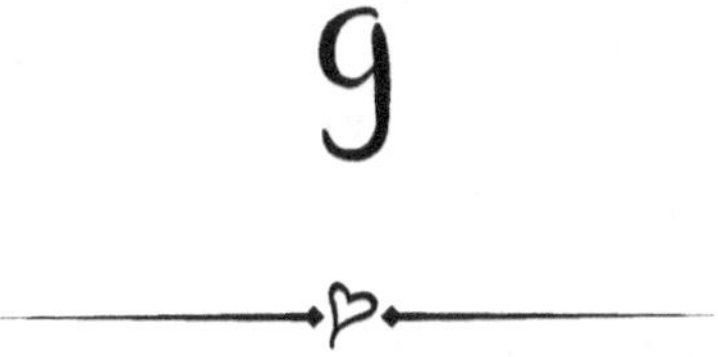

9

From a very young age, my sister and I were expected to excel academically. Growing up in an Indian household, the bar was set high; we were supposed to not just compete but consistently score above 90. However, I always found myself dwelling comfortably in the 70s, an average range that neither brought extreme happiness nor profound disappointment. In this world, a 90 is the pinnacle of success, worthy of praise. And, of course, my sister is the embodiment of perfection, excelling in everything, particularly in her studies. Our parents always manage to draw comparisons between us, and every time, she outshines me by a significant margin.

The constant comparison was an ever-present shadow that loomed over my academic journey. It wasn't just about personal growth or fulfilling my potential; it was about measuring up to an almost unattainable standard set by my sister's remarkable achievements. The pressure to perform was unrelenting, the competition was unyielding, and the expectations, at times, felt stifling. In a household where success was synonymous with academic excellence.

I had grown accustomed to this relentless cycle of competition and comparison, but lately, it has become unbearable. I yearned for the recognition and affection from my parents that they so readily showered upon my sister whenever she proudly presented her straight A's. This time, I was determined to earn those good marks.

I understood that when I received bad grades, it wasn't just disappointment; it felt like my parents harboured a genuine dislike for me. I was the product of their teachings and expectations, and if I turned out to be a poor student, it would amplify their burdens and troubles. That was the last thing I wanted.

Over that thought, my teacher specifically reached out to me, telling me that I was going down as an average scorer. I knew my scores from the '70s, but if they fell even more, the prospect of facing the worst scoldings from my parents if my grades dropped further was a terrifying thought. I understood that in order to study effectively, I needed an environment free of distractions, a space where I could immerse myself in the subject matter with unwavering concentration. Math, with its complex equations and challenging problems, had become my immediate battleground.

I sat at my desk, staring intently at the math textbook in front of me. In my head, the equations and numbers merged to form an impossible maze. The pain in my brain was from frustration. Why did I find this so difficult? If my sister can do it, why can't I? I thought. It was unbelievable; I couldn't understand anything; my brain was just now working. The digits from my book were contrasting, and it was all together. It was all cluttered, and I became dizzy. It was like the world was revolving, but at the centre was just me, this book, and all the unsolved problems waiting for me one by one.

The clutter was getting bigger and bigger when suddenly, my parents shouted my name. I quickly shut my book and rushed down to find them in the living room with a stern look on their faces. My mom and dad were already having a conversation with my elder sister, and she was smiling at them. "Sit down, Ruhi, my mom said. I took a seat next to my sister, who was smirking, almost as if she knew what was going to happen next.

My mom had started to say that it was the exam period, and we needed to buckle up, as it was a crucial time for all of us. Suddenly, her tone became serious. Ruhi This is the note you gave us from your teacher. Read it and let us know what you think. My mind had become still. Panic and frustration immediately came over me. I didn't know what was going to happen, but all I knew was that I was in grave peril, and this time I couldn't get out of it.

My mom reached out for the note, and I took it from her in shaky hands. I could feel eyes on me, and I didn't know what to do for them to look away. I opened the letter and read it.

It read:

Dear parent,

We would like to discuss Ruhi's academic and classroom progress. I would like to keep the parent well-informed about their child's growth and misconceptions. It would be great if we could discuss this matter in an in-person meeting and if we could have both parents present.

Please let us know your availability, and we will arrange a suitable time for the meeting.

Regards,
Mrs. Anu

After I was done reading, I looked up and saw three sets of eyes on me. My mind was dizzy; I didn't know what to say. My dad stepped in, noticing my anxiousness. "Do you know anything about that? Dread washed over me, and I felt a knot form in my stomach. I was indeed anxious, but my confusion ran deep as well. What was this about? Could it be because I hadn't been paying much attention in class? Or perhaps because I rarely participated in discussions, never raising my hand to answer questions? Or was it connected to the morning incident with Mrs. Anu? Come to think of it, she was quite mad, and she called me to her desk after that.

I knew if I said I didn't, I would get more scolding, and conflicts would arise. I didn't want that. So I simply said, "I think I may have some sort of idea." My parents looked taken aback, but my sister was grinning, almost as if she was enjoying this.

"Ruhi, If there's anything going on in school, you know you can tell us, right?" My mom's voice quivered with concern. Her words surprised me, as I hadn't expected them to handle the situation so well.

However, deep down, I couldn't shake the feeling that this was somehow connected to my sister, the only one in our family who seemed to hold my parents' undivided attention. I locked eyes with her, suspicion creeping in. She had a motive, I thought, though I couldn't fathom what it might be. She glanced at our parents and then back at me, her expression inscrutable.

My head felt like it was spinning, and I struggled to keep my composure. My eyes welled up with tears, and I battled the urge to cry out for help. The pressure and confusion were becoming overwhelming.

Summoning my remaining strength, I took a final, shaky breath and replied, "Nothing is going on. I have to go." Without waiting for their response, I bolted from the room and sprinted up the stairs, desperately seeking refuge in my bedroom.

I needed to escape. I didn't want to think about this entire situation, but I just couldn't stop imagining everything that would happen when we met my teacher. The mere thought of the disappointment in my family's eyes and the disapproval from society sent shivers down my spine.

It was all too much; I was hyperventilating and gasping for breath, and I didn't want my parents to see me in this state. I was too tired to go downstairs. I knew right now that there was something that could possibly worsen my state and their worries if I went down like this. So, I skipped dinner, washed my face, and went to bed. I would deal with the world, the troubles, and the burdens tomorrow.

Right now, I just want to *get away.*

10

I was extremely scared for the next morning. I woke up in a sullen manner. I just wanted to get away from here, remove myself from this situation, and go far away to somewhere where I could concentrate and focus. I knew when I went down, my parents would force me into a conversation, and my mind would spiral and trail off all over again. Standing on the bathroom floor, looking up at the mirror, yet again made me feel so many different things. I am here when I'm insecure when I'm sad, happy, excited, and anxious. Today, I was going to go through it again.

I told myself everything would be alright and prepared to go down. As I was making my way to the stairs, I passed my sister's room. I was angry. I knew she also hated the expectations that were cast upon her during the exam period, but she had absolutely no right to change her attitude and the wrath of my parents and direct it towards me.

I stepped into her room and looked directly at her. I saw her eyes slowly turn and find it's up to mine. I had no exact reason to be mad at her, but I knew for a fact that she was the one who knew what was going to happen.

I looked away. I was scared that if I said something, one thing would lead to the other, and another big conflict would take place, and I could not deal with so many emotions at once. I just left her room and slowly made my way down the stairs. I was so anxious and worried, and that's why I couldn't think straight. My parents definitely had something or another planned for me, and I didn't want to see how it was going to turn out.

As I descended the stairs, each step felt heavier than the last. The weight of anticipation seemed to consume me, making it difficult to breathe. I could hear my parents' hushed voices coming from the living room, their whispers carrying an uneasy tension. It was as if the very air in the house was charged with unspoken expectations and impending doom.

As I reached the bottom of the staircase, I could feel my heart pounding in my chest. I dreaded what awaited me in that room—the endless barrage of questions and comparisons that were sure to follow. It felt suffocating—this constant need to measure up to some ideal that had been imposed upon us.

But as I stepped into the living room, ready to face the storm, I was taken aback by what I saw. Instead of angry gazes and sharp words, there was an unexpected calmness settling over the room.

My parents were sitting on the sofa, their faces weary yet somehow understanding. It was as if they had momentarily set aside their own expectations and were now ready to listen.

I cautiously took a seat, unsure of what was about to happen. My mother broke the silence, her voice filled with a mix of concern and love. She spoke softly, her words like gentle waves washing over me. "We know how difficult this period is for you, dear," she said. "And we understand that you're feeling overwhelmed. But we want you to know that we're here for you, no matter what; we were just worried about your future."

Her words, unexpected as they were, touched a place deep within me. The emotions that had been brewing inside me suddenly spilled over, and tears welled up in my eyes. It was a torrent of relief and vulnerability, a release I didn't know I needed. At that moment, I felt a glimmer of hope amidst the chaos.

With every word she took, I kept wondering if this was the type of behaviour that would be present with them all the time or not. I could see my parents were getting impatient that I wasn't answering. All I wanted to tell them was that everything was alright and I didn't need their help. But I did need their help. I needed someone to get me out of this suppressed reality. It was suffocating, and maybe they could help me with it.

"No, everything is alright," I said, holding back those heavy tears that were slowly flooding my eyes. I could feel the atmosphere change. Both my parents were truly getting mad. They didn't understand that if I told them everything, they would just ask me to stop overreacting.

My dad spoke, this time in a very serious voice. "We do not accept this sort of behaviour in our house, Ruhi."

Ruhi, that broke my heart. My dad always called me by my nickname and never by my own name. I was scared now. I knew I was in deep trouble, but I could not handle this sort of tone from my dad. He was always there for me when my mom and I had conflicts. Whenever he and I fought, he still called me my nickname. I never once thought that he would say Ruhi unless he was genuinely serious.

"I understand, papa," I said in a soft manner. I had to be conscious of everything, especially my studies. Even though it was all too much, I had to concentrate.

I berated myself for being too thoughtless and not understanding all the situations going on at home. My heart felt so heavy that one of the tears flopped down from my eyes and made its way to my cheek.

I noticed my mom's hands turned into tiny fists. She hated it when my dad was angry. She knew that my dad was the problem solver and the one who was the happy, kind, and joyful soul in the house. So, when he gets angry, it is for a good reason. My mom slowly said, "You don't need to cry for this. It is a trivial matter, but if anything were to happen, There will be consequences."

"I understand, Mom." I wiped the tears from my face and watched as my mom went off to the kitchen to get started on breakfast, and my dad sat on the same couch, in that position, reading a newspaper. The air around the room had started to close in on me, and the chair I was sitting on felt like a bed of needles. They had acted like nothing had happened. I knew it was my fault. I wanted to say something, but I couldn't. I blinked and felt the water that was forming in my eyes.

I could no longer handle the symphony in the room. The bitter remarks and heated words are still hanging in the air. I needed to leave; my legs were wobbling and my hands were shaking, but I should not cry. I should not cry, I thought to myself. I could not let them see me like this, especially my mother. But whatever I do, I really need to get out of this room.

I immediately turned my back and faced the staircase. I shifted my weight to my other leg because it felt so wobbly, and I thought that I was going to injure it. The speed at which I was walking might have been slower than a tortoise.

My heart grew heavier as I made each step towards the staircase. I climbed the stairs, one agonising step at a time, while the walls appeared to close in around her. A torrent of ideas raced through her mind, and the wooden steps squeaked under her feet in unison. I couldn't handle it; it was all too much for me.

I deliberately forced my leg to hurry up and quickly made my way up the stairs. As I left, I could hear my parents' eyes on me. I went upstairs, letting out a huge sigh, as I wasn't in the sight of my parents anymore. I could hear a few murmurs coming from the living room. The tension inside me was immoderate. This was not normal; every time I had little control over my emotions, At this moment, my head felt dizzy, and I wanted to get away from this world. I knew that my mom told me not to cry, but I could feel a few drops coming out, and all I needed was to get to my room.

I couldn't help but wonder if my parents would have less trouble, fewer burdens, and one less disappointment in their lives. Should I be here? Or should I just go? I anticipated my very life. This was not the plan. But it all seemed so right.

It was like a battlefield; every step I took was much more dreadful than the last. My pace wasn't getting better, so with all the last energy I had left in my body, I wanted to go back to my room, get my phone, and watch either those cat videos or the pictures that would fill me up with memories. Anything, just anything, would be fine to remove me from this situation. I hated it.

I ran to my room, crying. It had all come out now, and even though I was asked not to, I couldn't help it. I pierced down and tried to take deep breaths, though I couldn't find my phone. I searched my room for my phone, and there was the knife that might have started or ended it all. I walked towards it, and it just happened so quickly. My vision was blurred, my legs felt rough, and I couldn't breathe. I tried calling out for help, but my voice felt heavy and my hands were numb. It just happened in under a second. I just couldn't think. My voice sank, and I passed out.

11

I cautiously opened my eyes in the clean hospital room and experienced an odd sense of bewilderment. I knew I was in a strange place when the air was filled with the strange smell of antiseptics and the gentle buzz of machines. I felt like my eyelashes were brushing across my cheeks, which helped me stay present.

As I blinked away the sleep haze, the room gradually became clearer. The soft light that was visible through the light blue curtains created a peaceful setting. The beeping from the heart monitor next to my bed appeared to sync up with the rapid heartbeat of my own worried body.

The IV line in my arm caught my attention since it was a visible reminder of my connection to this location. The fluid's cooling sensation stripped me of my body.

The events that had occurred before this point were shattered in memory, like shards of glass that needed to be put back together. There were hazy visions of sirens, bright lights, and urgent voices. Darkness followed a chasm that engulfed everything.

I turned my head cautiously, trying to get a better look at my surroundings. The clinical space was brightened by the colorful bunch of flowers on the windowsill. A chair that was unoccupied next to my bed suggested that someone had been there, keeping an eye on me while I was unconscious.

My fingertips brushed over a bandage on my forehead after I couldn't help but feel the desire to touch my face. That location was the source of a dull agony that demanded an explanation. A thirst for answers caused questions to flutter in my head like leaves caught in a soft breeze.

My room's door squeaked open, and a recognisable person walked in. It was my mother, who had eyes full of worry and relief—a delicate balancing act that only a mother could express so beautifully. Her eyes met mine, and I could see that she was both worried and appreciative as one tear made its way down her face.

She immediately made her way towards me and embraced me in a big hug. I could feel the warmth of her presence there, and it completed me; this was all I wanted, even though I struggled throughout.

I was still very confused by this shocking turnout of events. I did not know how I ended up here. All I knew was that sickening feeling of me questioning myself alive in this world. I slowly pieced all my questions together as the rest of my family made their way into the room.

Slowly, each of them hugged me one by one and asked me what happened and why I was there. My mom started, "Darling, we are so sorry; we didn't know how much pressure we were putting on you." I stared at her. I knew all the pain that had begun was not coming only from my parents but from our entire family.

All the rude and unnecessary comments that had started from a very young age had absolutely broken me into pieces. I think it was the big fight I had with my parents that was the last straw for me.

"But... I don't understand; how did I end up here?" I asked with a genuine curiosity in my tone. "Well, we asked Esha to go to your room and check on you to see if you were doing okay. Luckily, you didn't lock your door, and when she went in, she found you fainted on the floor. We immediately rushed you to the hospital, not knowing what to do next. We are deeply sorry, darling. We truly did not understand all the pain that you have been going through, and we just put more burdens on top of your head."

My mom gripped my hand, and at that moment, I instantly felt better. All I wanted was just somebody—a guide, perhaps—overseeing and escorting me towards all the good and happy moments in my life. My mom smiled at me as tears fled from her eyes. My sister and dad were staring at me from the side with their sad eyes.

Right then, a nurse came beside me and corrected the pillow placement, so I would no longer lay down but instead stand upright in a less comfortable position. The nurse then muttered something to my family, and all of them came to one side of the bed while the door was gently flung open.

A doctor walked in. She was elegantly moving. Her stance exuded warmth and professionalism at the same time. She was a mature woman who instantly put me at ease with her calm demeanor. Her perceptive, hazel eyes seemed to be able to peer without bias into the darkest recesses of your soul.

Her face was framed by loose waves in her chestnut hair, which added to her friendly demeanor. Her hair was streaked with streaks of silver. She exuded a certain amount of confidence, but it was matched by an evident compassion that seemed to come from within her. She had the kindest eyes and a small smile on her face as she made her way in with a few papers on a clipboard.

"Hello, my name is Dr. Rashmi Sharma. I am a mental health

specialist, and I am here after running a few tests on you." I looked at my mother in complete panic. What was going to happen? Was she going to give me good or bad news? Will my parents get panicked by more bad news, or is everything going to be alright soon enough?

"I know you must be thinking about the worst possible outcomes when you hear the word 'tests', but rest assured, everything is alright. I would just like to get all of your attention for a few minutes, please." She then made sure that everyone's eyes were on her, including mine, and then she began.

"As you all know, from a certain age group, all of our concerns start. Whether it has to do with our weight, height, appearance, expenditure, bills, studies, etc.

But, in today's world, this stress and concern that had been weighing on all our shoulders at adulthood is starting from very young ages, childhood, or teenhood." She looked at me and then continued. "Sometimes this worry and anxiety can get to our minds so much that it could affect us both inside and out. It could absolutely inflict so much pain in our lives that we do not know what to do or where to go."

"Ruhi is one of the cases, or rather, an example of what I am conversing with you all." I could feel everyone's eyes on me, and I nodded along with what she said, a sense of familiarity from the soft tone of the words she said. I understood, and I could relate to all the circumstances she mentioned.

"Did you ever feel this sort of way, ever, in these past few weeks, or months, perhaps?" For a while, I thought, and the silence in the room foreshadowed me.

I took a deep breath and answered, "Yes, I have." I could feel the eyes of concern cast upon me. My mom and dad looked at each other, and my sister's face looked shocked.

"That's all I wanted. A lot of people who are going through such horrendous states tend to find comfort in a lot of different activities and turn to the state of their room, as it brings them a lot of joy."

"I suppose she has been doing the same thing." I nodded at her, wondering how she could understand every one of my experiences, comprehend them, and put them into words so carefully and in such a heightening and appealing way.

"So, would you like to explain all your problems to them in a soft manner? You don't have to rush, and no one is going to judge you, so don't worry."

I was ready. At that moment, I didn't think that there were eyes on me or that everyone was going to judge me for what I was going to say. But I thought that these were my family members, who had seen every phase of my life since I was young.

I took a few seconds and finally started speaking. I explained my problems from the start and how, in those circumstances, I experienced episodes of shaking hands, wobbling legs, a lump in my throat, etc. I described every horrible situation I was a part of and how my feelings were.

With each and every word I muttered, I felt like there was a weight being lifted off my shoulders as I was sharing my voice with my loved ones, who would always be there for me, even at my worst times.

When I was done, I looked up from my hands and up at my family members, who looked broken. I could imagine all the thoughts that must have been thrown at them. This was all very new to them, and

I just couldn't imagine how they were feeling at this point in time.

There was an awkward silence for a moment, and I signalled to the doctor to take over. She opened her mouth and started saying, "This is just one of the many cases that happen in every child. It is a long process, and it cannot fully be healed, but some of the symptoms could be gone, and that's what matters most. I think she should start therapy; it's a good process, and it will definitely help and heal her."

My parents looked at each other and at me. I so badly wanted to get up from the bed and tell them that I knew therapy was the best choice for me.

My sister was looking at me with apologetic eyes; she knew that that day I was there to talk to her and resolve things with her. I could feel it. The entire ambiance of the room changed. I didn't know if things were going to be resolved, but all I knew was that it was all going to end up in positive and good circumstances because I would work towards it and make it happen.

It had only been a few weeks since I started therapy. It was a mix of a lot of feelings: anticipation, anxiety, and hope. I couldn't help but wonder if everything was going to be alright now or if I was still going to get all those episodes where I was completely helpless and where my mind felt dizzy.

My family had realised that therapy was the best for me, and I could get the most out of it. I loved therapy. Every minute of it. It was so enlightening to talk to someone of such strength. She guided me through all my problems and suggested effective methods that might free me from this torture.

I was doing much better in school, too. We already had the meeting for the note, and it turns out Mrs. Anu had nothing bad to say about me except that my studies were missing a factor of interest. I used to be really interested in whatever she had to say, but these days I was off in my own world.

I had developed an interest in my sessions in therapy. Due to the help I got, I had built up so many things that I lost them while I was battling this problem of mental health.

I was happy. For a long time, my thoughts were always suppressed and never heard. This mindset affected my life to the brim, and therapy controlled it to the point where I got my old life back. I have a completely new mindset now. With the help of others, especially my family,

After the sudden confrontation with my sister at the hospital, she realised that none of us were being our true selves, and we needed to talk things out. We sat together, and I told her all the mixed emotions and the flooding feelings that suddenly flushed in when I used to face something bad. It was nice to talk to her again.

She understood all my problems and told me that her teenage years weren't as good as she projected them to be.

I slowly resolved all my problems one by one, as my therapist mentioned. I was lacking in communication and speech, and for it to be right, I needed to practice keeping my emotions and feelings in order.

I still had conflicts and still had those episodes where I just wanted to give up and get away from the world. But with the comfort and love of my family members, I felt safe, and I knew I could tackle all that came upon me.

Due to this newly prominent mindset, I started being mindful of myself and all those around me. I learned that true love and acceptance should first come from myself, and I should never try to compare myself with others.

Slowly, I started gaining interest in all of my old hobbies. I missed doing art and listening to music. I realised that, at a slow pace, I could work with anything and build it up to finally complete it.

When I first started therapy, I could not identify any changes in myself, and I did not see much of a big impact. I felt anger arise when I realised that I still couldn't answer in class, talk to people, etc. Slowly, as I made my way through it, I realised that all I needed to do was take smaller and smaller steps towards my goal and ambition.

"You are the best thing." says Toni Morrison. The number of times I reviewed and read this lit a spark in me. I was always taught to keep others happy. My loved ones, family and friends, and even the people I meet—I never thought to myself that I could be the reason for my happiness.

Toni Morrison was another famous woman. She must have also gone through numerous struggles when she was my age, but it was so happening that she still fought through all the different comments pertaining to her. She was such an inspirational and aspirational woman, and she had written the quote I live by.

My therapist had asked me to view things from a side and asked me to write all my feelings in a book. She told me to vent out all the emotions and thoughts that were running through my mind when I was going through all of these circumstances. What's more, she told me to write down all of the circumstances to indicate a reminder of how far I have come. And how slowly I was going to work on myself and become the person I always wanted to be. To have that unconditional self-love towards myself.

I would work towards it. I knew that. In order to finally have a peaceful and calm state of mind, to work things out with others, and to be the person I want to be, I should love myself. I was going through my entire journey when I was writing down all the problems that I experienced.

I realised that my entire journey had been a combination of turns and turns and every potentially awful emotion I had ever had. I also went through a lot of backlash from different people. Due to this task of journaling, I saw all the positive and negative attributes in my life, the people who support me, and the people who withhold me from flying away and rising high.

I had changed so much, and I just thought about that. From the most nervous and awful state, where I felt empty and unloved, to a much more unique state, where I was treading very lightly because each comment had absolutely broken me.

To all the conflicts and fights I had with people around me. Including myself. Then, due to the very harmful experience, I had by vigorously applying chemicals to my face and starving myself without a clear guide,

To a more relaxing yet horrendous state where I did receive a lot of backlash and hurtful comments, but a few of my family members were right there for me.

To the point where I knew that therapy was the best option for me but was still neglected and turned away from my own family members. I was in the most vulnerable stage, and I did not see that my own family would have the guts to take care of my own upcoming needs.

I should have realised that they should not be able to make every single decision for me. I could not have more people line up and step on my decisions that I knew would be the best option for me.

At the end of the day, I know myself the most because nobody has been in my place and dealt with the exact same things that I have. There are a lot of people who could relate and give me advice. But true, significant changes would have to come from me because I am doing this for myself.

After the stage of being neglected by my own family, where they wouldn't hear my thoughts, I decided to silence myself completely anyway.

I didn't speak in class anymore, and this affected my participation and listening skills. My teachers slowly realised that my spark, my interest, and the position held for me in my studies were suddenly destructing, and I had none of that anymore.

I had completely lost interest and was in this world where I could be myself, except that it was just my imagination and intrusive thoughts.

Then the situation was that my teacher caught that sudden lack of attention during classes and immediately whisked me off to private talks with my parents. The pressure and the weight of the burdens had drawn such a heavy weight on my shoulders that I couldn't take it anymore. I ended up in the hospital, where I could finally voice my thoughts, and people were actually willing to listen to me.

During this entire voyage, I ended up in the greatest and most comfortable place I have ever been. It got into my thoughts and changed my perspectives and the way I think and speak indefinitely. I could voice my thoughts properly now, and all the other features that I needed to work on were slowly building a path and finally making me happy!

13

I looked out the window, pondering the tiniest details of life. I didn't realise how much education was important, but it didn't really matter if I was going to pay attention now or not. It was the end of the year anyway. I was smiling at my book, as I had made a small flower there and I wanted to make it better.

My teacher had written a few things on the board, and she was talking while I stared out the window. I looked outside, and the view was giving me a sense of deja vu. The same serene plants, trees, and wind swaying against the gardens, like at the start of my journey.

But something was different. I noticed the previously unbloomed flower had blossomed into the most wonderful thing I'd ever seen. It was growing, and it fit around the rest of the leaves, beautiful in its own way. It was no longer suppressed by its own leaves, and it was free to grow and be stronger with the help of the sunlight. That flower is me, I thought.

No longer suppressed. No longer sad, and shunned away from all around it. I smiled to myself. I remember all the emotions and feelings that passed by me in this awful yet beneficial phase. I had sat at the very same desk, with the very same view, with the very same teacher and the batch of students, and with the same old discussions that had been going on for a long while. But I was not the same person. I had a different mindset and a different thinking system. The way I viewed and grasped every little thing in life was different.

And I am happy to say that it is so good to not have my emotions get the better of me. It is so good to let myself blossom and move freely in the way I want and not in the way others might want me to. I knew that I had come a long way from all the trouble I had faced. I was happy to embrace all my flaws now. I had come to a situation where I knew that my flaws and all the other things that I knew made me insecure were there for a reason. It made me stand out. And every single human should not be the same, and this was the thing that made me stand out.

The way my world had entirely changed after this circumstance It had been about 6 months into therapy now, and I had really learned to spread my wings and embrace all that I was insecure about. My research has also proven to be right. The power of therapy indeed did work, and I was not using this as a scheme to spend more money, as I did on the products, as my aunt so lovingly mentioned.

My family had also found out about my turn of events, even though they had a fair share of things to say. They were still happy that I finally poured my heart out and was getting the help I needed. For my family, I was a lot. I knew I was a burden to all of them, so I learned to stand on two feet alone. I was proud. Of how far I have come and, mainly, of myself. I looked back and laughed at all the intrusive thoughts I had. I couldn't help but wonder how lost I was at that point in time. I was always lost in thought about everything.

I wasn't lost in thought anymore; instead, I was lost in a world of introspection, where the simple beauty of an unopened flower symbolised my ongoing quest for self-discovery and acceptance. To embrace my flaws, I had to love the entire output. After all, my imperfections made me perfect. So, in a way, I am imperfectly perfect; we all are!

Epilogue

This message was dedicated to each and every person who was struggling with this sort of situation, and everyone beyond that too. I grew up in an Indian household and did not have it easy either. This book was solely based on all of my family members and friends who have gone through this. I wanted to make more people aware of this sort of issue, which looks very minor but is not. I wish that everybody who has faced this problem has found solutions and is now living in a less toxic and hurtful environment. I really hope that I have helped you, even if it is in the smallest way possible. It is not easy being a teenager and living in such an unfair world. I hope the message was conveyed. You are perfect, just the way you are!

THANK YOU!

www.ingramcontent.com/pod-product-compliance
Lightning Source LLC
Chambersburg PA
CBHW020933160726
47993CB00007B/2770